This book is for Agnes Cullen,
my nana, who I loved with all my heart. She is
missed always, until we meet again.
Also for my mother, who without I would be
lost, she gifted me with storytelling.
And my beloved children Maria, Johnjoe, Kielan,
Kristian, Michael-Darragh, Leo, and Declan. All of
you are the stars I carry inside of my heart, ever
shining and bright, filling my life with joy and
love.
Lastly for you Ger, for the road ahead will no
doubt be rocky. But if you never let go of my
hand,
I promise to hold onto yours forever.
XXXXXXXXXXXXXXXXXXXXXX

Chapter 1
Before Our Time!

Ask yourself this question, have you ever felt like someone or something was watching you. Even if it's on a sunny day, at lunch time and you're surrounded by family and friends while out on a picnic. When what you're getting creeped out by, appears to anyone else to simply be a tree? If the answer is yes, then you are like me and you have been told of the secrets of the Tree-Witches and have been shown all of the hidden signs of their past punishments.

This here is my journal, where I keep all my fears and hopes - a place I can always come to and write down all of my thoughts and plans for the future. But it's also a book about those secret Tree-Witches and when the time is right, I will share all that I know with the world!

Hi, my name is Kirah Dove and I'm eleven years old, today, on the 16th of march, the year is 2014. My wonderfully old, wise know-it-all grandmother has at long last passed on all of her knowledge and secrets and also her fears of the Tree-Witches. So this is my warning, if you are of a gentle nature and steer away from stories of evil witches and black magic, this is not a tale for you. So put this book down and carry on with your carefree life and childhood. I wish you all every happiness and good luck for the future (you will need it). But if you, like me, are a true seeker of the truth, of all that lies behind the tales of old, then my friends, read on and know I speak the truth to you. I do so at great risk and I beg of you to use this knowledge wisely.

I was about five years old when I first realised that not all trees are, just that, trees! But many are in fact witches from the past that have been punished for crimes of old and turned into the most sinister of trees. My Irish grandmother, Annie, came to live here (in Northamptonshire) many years ago in the sixties, at the age of 14. She brought with her the tales of past wars that she would never be able to tell anyone who would truly believe her, until now!

They are not like the wars we learn all about in school, like the First World War or the Second, where men fought and died for our freedom, or even the earlier battles, like the War of the Roses or the Battle of Hastings. No, the war stories of which her own great grandfather swore her to silence, are so very much older. My sweet old grandmother learnt of a very different war and many battles of a secret kind, that only by her recollection, a handful of people from each country in the world knew about or even less likely, know about now.

The only reason she confessed all this to me, was because, after years of gathering information on those times (and through recovering many stories of the witches from that era), she has come to the conclusion, that by her great-grandfathers calculations (and those of his forefathers), that the year 2015, is the year all witches will be released from the spell that was placed on them a thousand years ago (could this all possibly be true!). Am I to believe that everything I have been told is true and not simply a bedtime story? I just have to find a way to warn others who, like me, already know or suspect or who would, when told, believe it too, that next year, will be the most dangerous year in our history. Then that way, I could make a plan and have allies too. I feel kind of at a loss, I know I can't do this alone, so brave as I might sound, I'm very much afraid and any day now, the bright light of my world will leave this world for the next.

That light of which I speak, is my dear grandmother, whom I have already told you about. She came to live with me and my older brother, David, after we lost both our parents in a tragic car crash nine years ago. I was just a baby, not even one; my brother David, was twelve years at the time and never speaks of it. We were so lucky to have survived the crash that took our parents' lives; "a miracle" said the Fire and Rescue Team. But that crash took our parents and any chance for me to get to know them.

Our grandmother, Annie, travelled by boat from Ireland as soon as she heard the news. She would have flown over, but she didn't own a passport - and still doesn't to this day. She, you see, had long since moved back to Ireland, well before my brother was born. I know that my parents took my brother over to Ireland many times and even me once, for summer holidays. I have seen some old photos of those summers in an old scrapbook that my brother keeps well hidden away; he can't bear to look at them. I feel his pain and sorrow so much, both me and nana know where he hides them (under his bed) and we often get them out and spend hours looking through all the pictures. She would delight in telling me how much my father loved my mother and what a beautiful person inside and out she was. Nana would describe how kind and gentle my father was and how my parents had so many friends - people just loved to be around them.

I wouldn't have known much about my parents if I didn't have nana. My brother (as I said before) has never been able to talk about it and from what my nana has said, he has pushed those who once knew our parents out of our lives, all except nana. Even nana knows better than to speak about them around him.

David seems so sad sometimes, like he carries the weight of the world on his young shoulders. He has always been a kind, gentle brother and I have so many wonderful memories of us together. He taught me to whistle and ride my bike, which he saved up for with his own paper round money. He had me riding that beautiful, baby pink bike at the age of three without the stabilisers (pretty good, hey?). My nana told me he is so much like our father in nature and looks and I see it too from the hidden photos.

My only wish is that one day, David will be ready and he will sit me down, in our favourite corner of the house, where he loves to read to me all kinds of stories and tales on rainy days. David has never believed in granny's tales of the Tree-Witches and has, over the years, warned me not to take her so seriously.

David has heard nana's tales all his life and only ever believed her once, he told me he was about five and he would have sworn to the Queen of England that he had seen his nana talking to animals. But in this case, he swears that the animals were talking back to her, a lizard, I think he said it was. I used to love listening to this story of his about her. He always loved to make out that our nana had special powers. I, myself, have wondered, as often, my nana will seek to be alone for hours in her room or go out on lonely walks by herself. I've thought, many times, that she was talking to someone else in her room or whilst in the garden. But whenever I would burst in on her, over the years, she was always alone. David, I know, adores his nana, but things change and now he's a grown man of twenty-one.

David has a beautiful girlfriend called Claire, she wants to be an ambulance driver and is already in training; she is the sweetest person we know and so different to my brother. Where

David is quite straight and sensible, she is completely mad and so funny - she makes us laugh all the time with the things that come out of her mouth. You won't believe it, but she once got a tattoo on the back of her neck, of an elephant, because she loves them. But to her bad luck, due to the tattoo artist's bad eyesight, she ended up with an elephant whose trunk resembled a little boy's winky (if you catch my drift)! She cried about it for a few days, then told everyone and gave us all a huge laugh. Later on, she got it removed (once she could afford to). I've grown to love her so much, she is like my best friend and big sister all rolled into one.

David and Claire have been going out together since they first met four years ago. They were both just seventeen years old at the time. Apparently they fell in love whilst trying to hit each other one night at a fair ground, while driving their bumper cars into each other. Claire has always told me, that she believes one day, David will open up about our parents and that this could be at any time. We made a promise that we would be there for him whenever this happens. He's always been there for both of us - helping bring me up since I was a baby, he's also supported Claire through her parents' divorce and ambulance training.

Just the four of us live here together in a very small village called Nobottle. The village lies on the outskirts of Northampton Town. It is in fact a hamlet, which of course, are very rare and Nobottle is one of the smallest hamlets in England. To get to our village, you must use a really old Roman road. It's very quiet here, but very beautiful. We live in a small, seen-better-days, tiny, thatched cottage, that my father inherited from a crazy old aunt of his - who loved cows and kept five as pets.

My father sold them all to a local farmer, then changed his mind and brought them all back again to be kept as his pets, even after they stopped giving milk. We still have two of them now, named Batman and Robin. We all know that they are female cows and our dad would have known this too. He must have been such a character, giving his cows such silly names. I wish I could have known him just for a day. I would have loved, so much, to hear the sound of his voice when he called to those two cows. They, apparently, would always come running when they heard him call - my nana, while laughing her small head off, told me so.

My mother loved it here, my nana told me. My mother loved to go horse riding nearby in the countryside and go for long romantic walks with my father. They were even known, in this very tiny village, to go for moonlit walks when they first moved here, before me and my brother were born.

The few that live here always carry that sad smile on their faces whenever they see us. My nana explained to me long ago that they don't mean any harm, that they just can't help it. "Your parents were so popular and thought of." She always knows just what to say and how to put things. She brings such a peace with her. I can never remember her being really cross or mad about anything. She has always been there to explain things and to give me and my brother the warmest and biggest hugs.

I don't know what life is going to be like without her and its breaking my heart that I will have to say goodbye to her soon. My nana is the only mother I have ever known. The doctors have said she is riddled with cancer and that it's really just a waiting game now. She has so many pills to take for the pain and she sleeps most of the time now. But she made me promise to write her tales down and to keep a diary of my life.

Every day I watch her get weaker and every day she tells me a bit more. I know she is trying to prepare me for what lies ahead. I find it hard to pray, I'm scared and angry with God that he should take my nana from me. I feel bad because I know in heaven she will be in pain no more.

30thof March 2014
Dear Journal,

So Here I am sitting in her room watching her sleeping and listening to her shallow breathing. I'll get her story all written down as best as I can and remember. She has given me her rusty old key to her ancient worn out trunk that resembles a treasure chest from pirate days gone by. This chest has in it, every single account and link that she has made through her sixty year search. She has shown me many things from it before, although I do remember there was one book in there, she would never let me read or see. You could say she even acted as though she was afraid of it. I will wait till she is at rest before I go looking (or snooping), I have promised myself.

26th of April 2014
Dear Journal,

It's been many weeks now and nana is getting frailer and frailer as the weeks go by. So I need to explain it all to you from the start, so let us go back and begin with what would be my great-great-grandfathers' tales and stories that he passed onto my nana.

His name was Bartholomew Keating. He lived till he was one hundred and seven years old and my nana adored him. He told her that the days of old hid a forgotten secret. A secret about the lives and times of those few women, who worshipped the dark side, THE DEVIL! And took part in the dark one's magical rituals and sacrifice - every week, when they would travel twenty miles on a pony and trap to visit him, he would tell my nana a little more.

His wife was forever telling him to stop telling tales and to leave my poor nana alone, but she loved to hear his stories and always believed them to be just that - until at his death bed. He asked to be left alone with his great-granddaughter, Annie. He explained that everything he ever told her was the absolute truth and she must, for the sake of both their ancestors, believe him.

He told her how much he loved her and didn't mean to scare her, but it was his duty to pass the knowledge to another member of the family. Knowing his own sons and daughters would not believe him, and think him crazy, if he was to claim that all his bedtime stories were in fact the truth. They, for sure, would ignore it as the ramblings of an old confused man. He knew with her he had a chance, that she, like him, had the gift of knowing when a lie was being told.

He begged her to believe and he died with a smile on his face as she held his hand. He knew that he needn't have worried, she believed him and would one day too, pass on the truth to her own children. But of course her children thought that they were just very good bedtime stories.

The man she married was an English man named James Robinson, who would laugh at her crazy stories and tell her to stop scaring the children. My nana's husband died shortly after my mother turned seven, so after her children were grown up and had met their partners, she moved back to Ireland to research more and to gather all she could on witchcraft in Ireland. There she waited for the grandchildren to be born and would try her luck with them and hit bingo with me.

The first thing my nana told me was to be very careful with whom I share this knowledge. The last thing she wanted was to see me lose good friends, as very few would believe. She didn't want me to have everyone stare, like I was some crazy person or worse, the village idiot!

The only friends I have shared this secret with are Kristian and Jack - though they believe it to be make-believe. They are first cousins that live on a farm a couple of miles away. Grace and Isabelle are sisters who live over the road in the grandest house by far in our petite village. Their father is a very wealthy man indeed; their mother is a hippy chick, women's rights activist who lets her girls do whatever they like. They can at times, be really annoying because they are so spoilt, but nana told me to be tolerant though firm with them.

I could be a good role model for them, because the fact is, they get so bored with each other's company and we all live so far from any exciting shops or anything modern, like the cinema. They never like to fall out with me and usually they behave themselves and they have always loved my nana's stories, even if they choose not to take them for fact.

Kristian would be my best friend out of all four of them, as he and I have a lot in common - he also lost his parents when he was very small. He was just four years old when his father died, he had been a soldier and served in Afghanistan. His mother then died from breast cancer only two years later.

He was sent to his uncle and aunt's farm to be raised by them, so he understands me, and he has confided in me so many times that he too believes the old tales are true. At first I thought he was just saying these things to be nice to me, but now I believe that he does really believe, like me.

We all love to discuss the Tree-Witches in my club-house that my brother built for me with his own hands, four years ago. We are all getting a bit big for it now, but we love it in there. We have so many wonderful memories together - so many sleepover's and we would love to scare one another with made up tales of the Tree-Witches and, if the curse was ever lifted, what they would do for revenge. Sometimes we really would succeed in scaring the hell out of each other. So much so, that we would all end up huddled together and sleep on the bedroom floor in nana's room.

She would laugh and tell us we are right to be scared and being scared is a good thing; makes you quick on your feet and your senses keen and alert. Just perfect for running away from Tree-Witches.

She loves to tell her stories and have us as her captive audience. I am so afraid when she leaves me, that my world will begin to fill with darkness.

1st of May 2014
Dear Journal,

We are in May now, fast approaching my nana's 94th birthday! Will she make it to see her birthday - It's only a week away? I have made her something special for her birthday, I can't wait to give it to her. I pray that she will get to see it, and we can have a wonderful day.

Kristian has been such a great friend to me over the course of my nana's sickness. He has let me talk and talk till I'm blue in the face and have let all my feelings out. He said his uncle, Garfield, always says it's better out than in and not to bottle up all your feelings. Kristian makes me laugh and I know I'm very lucky to have a friend such as him. Sometimes I feel like I would like him to kiss me and then I feel very silly inside. We are just friends. I don't think Kristian will ever like me in that way. I'm just happy to have him and hope he never finds out how much I really like him.

I sometimes have this daydream that me and him will become, in the future, a modern day Hansel and Gretel witch hunters. We would be so famous and fall madly in love. It's my most favourite dream - that and finding lots of buried treasure in the garden.

Chapter 2
Goodbyes and Hellos!

8th May 2014
Dear Journal,

There is so much to do and so very little time, the doctor has been and gone and has told my brother that my nana has been asking for a priest. Today is her ninety-fourth birthday. We need to start making arrangements for her funeral, I can't think straight and I know my brother is the same. We were both, kind of, in denial for weeks, not believing that she could really be dying and leaving us all alone.

I think that's why she has held on for so long, she doesn't want to leave us because we are not ready. But you can never be ready to lose someone dear to you. Life isn't fair sometimes and you just have to be brave and strong, because really, you have no other choice. I must stay strong for David, thank goodness for Claire, she will help pull us through this sad time in our lives.

I have my friends too, I know I can especially rely on Kristian, because he has been through the same heartache. I watch my brother, his shoulders slumped, as he goes to ring Fr. John, the kindest priest you could ever wish to meet. I listen in on their conversation, I can hear Fr. John asking after me, he's worried about me. All of sudden, I freak out and run to be with my nana. This is really happening and she is dying and I need to be with her till the end. I need her to know just how much me and my brother love her.

Every last second I have with her is precious. Memories invade my mind of happy times with her in the past. I enter the room so quietly and turn; I see, to my surprise, that nana is sitting up in bed and smiling at me with her arms open wide. I run into them and cry my heart out. I can feel her soft and warm hand stroking my hair as she whispers, "I know darling, I know".

I pull out of my pocket the birthday gift I had only just finished drawing for her. It was a drawing of the Tree-Witches with a quote at the bottom saying, "I believe in The Tree- Witches!". My nana looks at the picture and smiles at me, "You know, you're a very good artist Kirah. I love it, thank you so much - and for always believing in me".

"I don't want you to die nana! I don't want you to leave us! I love you so much".

"I know darling and I would much rather stay here with you and your brother, who have loved me better than anyone else ever could".

"So why is God taking you when you don't even want to go and we need you here with us?"

"Now darling, don't be going blaming God and being all angry with Him, sure you know that my body is very old and weak now. I should have looked after myself better and stayed away from all those cream cakes that I love so much, they haven't been great for my heart and gave me a waist even Jabber the Hut would be jealous of".

"Stop trying to make me smile nana!"

"But you have such a beautiful smile and I sure do love to see it, now come now, dry them there tears of yours. I need you to do me a favour and be quick, before your brother comes in and brings Fr. John with him".

"What is it nana? What do you need me to do?"

"Child, I need you to go under my bed and pull out an old box of mine, it's right at the back and its wrapped in an old, green, woolly jumper".

"Okay nana, sure, no problem, what's it for?"

I was thinking she must have something special for me, that she wanted me to have, to keep after she passes away. Or maybe it could have been some money or maybe something of my mother's. I was quite excited to find out what it was, but 'my heart was still in the depths of despair' - a saying I learnt from my favourite book called Anne of Green Gables.

"Be real careful now you hear, don't pull it out too fast, just take your time and whatever you do, don't drop it!"

"Okay nana!"

Boy there seemed to be life in the old girl yet! It must be something really delicate, I thought, and easy to break or smash. What could it be? I had never in my eleven years of living in this cottage, ever come across this strange and unusual box. It looked like something out of the dark ages and it had patterned holes all over it. It was made from wood - which wood I don't know, as it had a colour I had never seen before. It was a kind of purple wood and was kind of heavy as well. I noted it was beautifully made, with love and care. I also noticed there were lots of crosses carved into it. I had never in my life seen such a box.

I was thinking that she was going to pass onto me yet another set of rosary beads; I had, like, five already from when I made my first holy communion. There is no way I would have ever guessed, in a million years, what was truly in that small box; but I was about to find out.

I handed the box gently to my nana, who placed it on her lap and then gestured for me to pass her the old, worn, woolly jumper and place it beside the box.

"Go check your brother's not coming".

I ran so quickly and checked, I could hear he was on the phone to Claire asking her how fast could she get back home.

"He's talking to Claire nana, so he could be a while".

"Good, that's great. Now, you come here, we have to do this fast as I can feel I'm getting weaker and I may not have the strength soon, and there is still so much to tell you and explain".

"What's inside the box nana that you don't want David to see?".

"There's something darling that I have kept from you. I have wanted to tell you for a long time now, but I promised to wait till the time was right. I'm sorry, don't think that I didn't trust you, but It wasn't up to me".

"I don't understand nana, what's in that box that you would have to keep it a secret and hidden away from me?"

I watched as she slowly opened the box and to my amazement, there, inside was a small newt. We hadn't that long ago learnt about them in school. I know that they live half their life in water, like ponds, hiding in deep mud and under rocks. Then, the other half, on land in the search of food; they eat meat and are known to some as salamanders.

"Why, oh why, does my nana have one of these?" I asked myself. "What a strange gift to leave me! What would I do with a newt?" I was feeling just a little disappointed; that was up until the moment I got a bit nearer and heard it speak! Yes that's right, you heard me, it spoke to me and this is what it said:

"Did no one ever tell you it's rude to stare?"

Well to say my mouth fell open, would be an understatement, to say the least.

"Be nice Fr. Marcimus, I know you were having your mid-morning snooze, but really! This is Kirah, my granddaughter, you remember, you have been looking forward to meeting her all these years".

"True, I do sincerely apologise. I hope you can find it in your heart to forgive a very old and cranky man".

Yes it's true to say that I simply just stood there, mouth still open wide for several minutes. I could still be there right now, only for something my nana said made me wake from the stupefied state I had found myself in.

"Nana, am I dreaming? But did that newt on your lap just speak to me? Oh and did you just call it Father?"

"It girl! Now who's being rude, I am no it."

"Dear child let me explain very quickly, as we don't have much time. This jolly, little fellow on my knee is my best friend. He was given to me by my great-grandfather, Bartholomew Keating, when I was little less than your age. His name is Fr. Marcimus, in his words he is a priest! He has been passed down from generation to generation in my family, all who swore an oath to keep him safe and protected, no matter what. I now am choosing you, Kirah, to look after my dear friend and protect him with your life".

"But nana are you insane, how on earth can he be a priest, what happened to him that he became a newt?"

"He will tell you all you need to know in good time. Time of which I have little of, so I beg for your forgiveness now, that I never shared this secret with you, until now. It's all to do with The Tree-Witches, but I made a promise not to tell you until the time was right. We both felt you were just too young and now we are trusting you with all the knowledge and truth you will soon have; please forgive your old nana".

"There's nothing to forgive nana, I understand completely and I will do all you ask of me and more, I won't let you down, I promise nana".

"I need you to go into my bathroom and get me my bottle of holy water on the shelf by the window and bring it back here".

"Okay nana I have it, what do you need me to do with it?".

"Pass it to Fr. Marcimus, he knows what to do, we talked about this many times".

"Talked about what nana?"

"Dear girl your grandmother wishes for me to give her the last rites, Annie where is the oil you got from Fr. John the last time he came to visit?"

"Kirah, will you reach again under my bed and you should see my jewellery box?".

"Here you are nana but I'm sorry, I don't mean to be rude again, but you're just a newt, how can you give my poor grandmother the last rites?".

"With your help young lady; now come around here and Annie, you open the box quickly now".

My nana pulled out a small looking, round tin, very much like the ones you can get lip gloss in. This, I already know, holds the special oil for the sick and dying, it's part of the ritual of the sacrament of the sick, for the ill or dying. You place it onto their foreheads whilst making the sign of the cross. I've seen this done in church many times.

"Now Kirah, I need you to open both the holy water and the oil and place some on your nana's forehead, then I will need you to lift me up in your hand carefully, so I can reach her and make the sign of the cross and say the prayers".

Then, looking tenderly at my nana, "Annie I want you to lie down and relax okay?"

"Wait Father, I just need to give something else to Kirah. Sweet Kirah, come here to me. Here, have this".

I watched my nana's eyes look down at her left hand. She started to twist off the only ring I ever remember her wearing, all the days of my life.

"This was my own wedding ring and I really would love you to have it, along with all of your mother's things. I have kept them safe for you". I could see happy tears in her old tired eyes, a lump rose in my throat.

"I love you child. You and your brother have brought me so much happiness. I know you and Fr. Marcimus will become fast friends, just as we did. You must always remember he is a very old man/newt and can be, at times, very bad tempered and cranky, but there is nothing in this world that he wouldn't do for this family. He will be all that you will need in the battle ahead. He holds great power, given to him by God himself, that will rid this world of these foul women of darkness. He will show no mercy against any Tree-Witches that may come back to life".

"I wish you could be here to see it nana".

"Darling, I do too, now come give your nana a kiss and cuddle".

I take her all in, her unique smell of honey and lemon and how warm she always feels. I make a mental picture, I want to remember this moment forever. I whisper in her ear suddenly, as now I have all these things I have to say.

"Tell my mum and dad I love them and I promise to make you all proud, you were the best nana a kid could ever wish for. Thank you for everything and for believing in me and trusting me with your secret. I love you to the moon and back nana, I'm going to miss you so much."

Tears were now silently falling down my face, as my nana lay back and smiled at me and closed her eyes.

I placed the holy water and then the oil on her forehead and, while holding Fr. Marcimus up close towards my nana as instructed, he made the sign of the cross on her wrinkled old forehead and said his prayers, all in Latin. I couldn't understand a word of it, but it did sound beautiful. Nana had her eyes closed the whole time. When he was finished, he asked me to take him closer and he gently kissed my nana on the head and I heard him whispering to her.

"Thank you Annie, what a dear friend you have been to me all these years. I will remember all the happy times we have spent together. It's breaking my heart to say goodbye to you. But, you know you can trust me to look after your granddaughter; I vow to protect her and David with my life. God bless you and I will keep you in my prayers".

I watched my nana smile as she listened to what he was saying, then all of a sudden, in walked my brother with Fr. John.

"Kirah, how is she? Has she said anything, or has she been asleep this whole time? Err Kirah, what's that in your hand?".

I didn't have time to hide the tiny newt, Fr. Marcimus, from my brother. I slowly opened my hand to reveal the talking newt, not knowing what else to do. But good old nana came to the rescue.

"Oh David, Kirah here just wanted to show me her new friend she found in the garden, look at him, he's a dear little newt, so he is. She wanted me to meet him, please don't be mad at her, she will need a friend when I'm gone, you understand".

Trust nana to lay it on thick. I opened up my hand for both David to see and Fr. John.

"Wow, he's a cute little fellow, isn't he?" said Fr. John.

I watched David and I could tell a million thoughts were running through his head, but he was not about to become that bad guy and tell me off and send me out of the room.

Fr. John thanked me for already getting the holy water and oil out. Me and David, along with Fr. Marcimus watched as he started to give nana the last rites. He was so softly spoken and gentle with nana; I had always really liked this priest. He is so kind hearted and he thought the world of our nana. We all stood back and watched as nana tried to make the sign of the cross. Fr. John told nana he will look out for David and I, he then said his own goodbyes.

David turned to me and whispered,

"Say your goodbyes now pet, as I don't think it will be very long now. Don't worry, you let yourself cry if you want to, you don't need to be brave."

Nana looked so warm and comfortable and still had a smile on her face. I wondered ' has she already gone or is she just quietly sleeping.' So I cuddled up to my nana again; I told her I loved her and then David joined me and kissed nana on the top of her head. I could see the tears in his eyes ready to pour out. I reached out quickly and took his hand in mine, I wanted him to know that I was there for him and he didn't need to be brave and hold it in.

"Nana you saved us," said David, "I will never forget the sacrifices you made, leaving your family to come back here again, to keep watch over us. I will never be able to thank you enough for always making Kirah and myself feel safe and so loved. You did all you could for us. I promise that I will try just as hard to make sure Kirah feels safe and loved, like you taught me."

Slowly the door behind us opens and my brother's girlfriend, Claire, was standing in the doorway with tears streaming down her face. Once David saw her, he couldn't hold it back any longer and ran into her waiting arms and cried inconsolably.

"Perfect timing as usual Claire" she coughs.

"You are an amazing young lady and my dear grandson is so lucky to have you in his life. You both, just keep loving each other the way you do and you're gonna make it for sure. Nana coughed again. David I'm so proud of you and you're going to make a wonderful father one day, I only ask one thing of you and that is to always stand by your little sister and always believe her whenever she confides in you." Nana coughed uncontrollably, I began to think she wouldn't stop.

"Kirah darling, just keep being the wonderful person that you are okay? And I will be watching you from above". Nana then looked up.

"Fathers, I thank you for all you have done for me and my family. I will be praying for your souls in heaven" and then nana closes her eyes. "I love you all, remember me and farewell". A few seconds later she was gone.

We all could see she had passed on and was now finally resting in peace. I still had Fr. Marcimus in my hand. I didn't think, I just did what was, to me, the most natural thing to do. I climbed up into my nana's bed and lay next to her and buried my face in her quilt, which smelt so strongly of lemon and honey, her smell.

Next, I feel my brother and Claire cuddle into me, with both their arms wrapped around us. We stayed like that, for what felt like hours. We didn't hear Fr. John leave. She was gone, my nana was dead and I didn't know if my heart could take any more of this pain. What would the future be like without her, who would I confide all my childish dreams and hopes to? She meant the world to me and my brother, our lives will be so very empty without her.

15th of May, 2014
Dear Journal,

Our nana passed away peacefully at 2.15pm on the 8th of May, surrounded by her loved ones. For her funeral five days later, David organised a horse-drawn carriage and invited all our neighbours and friends, who all turned out to show their support. Fr. John sang her favourite song, Danny Boy, as her coffin was lowered into the ground. He has the most amazing voice and there wasn't a dry eye anywhere to be seen. I looked down at the bright, yellow dress I was wearing; as I gazed at all the different colours everyone had on, I smiled. David had asked everyone if they would wear something bright and cheerful, as nana was the most bright and cheerful person you could meet. David chose to wear a big, purple jumper that nana had knitted for him many years before and it was still too big for him. I felt for Fr. Marcimus inside my pocket, even he was wearing a tiny, bright, red scarf. I knew all of my friends were standing right behind me. I felt someone take a hold of my hand, I knew before my eyes looked into his, it was Kristian, he was wearing a bright orange t-shirt and gave me a warm smile.

The sun shone on us all day. We invited everyone back to ours and had a BBQ and everyone shared their stories of nana. My brother, David, never asked me to get rid of the newt. He had no idea it was a priest from medieval times, but he seemed to be aware that I had grown very attached to it. Every day was a nightmare, to wake up and then remember nana wasn't with us anymore. I had wanted to share my secret that day with Kristian, wanted him to meet Fr. Marcimus; I hated keeping this all to myself. But Fr. Marcimus and I decided the time wasn't right yet to share this with either my friends or David and Claire.

I know that sometimes my brother comes in at night and checks on me, to make sure I'm safely sleeping, more importantly, that I'm still breathing. He's so worried that he might lose me too. I wish I could take away his pain and fear, it can't be easy for him and he's trying so hard to carry me through this hard time. I am so lucky to have such a wonderful older brother; I know that all through my life he will be looking out for me, as I will be looking out too, the best I can for him.

CHAPTER 3
Fr. Marcimus

13th of June 2014

Dear Journal,

It's been four weeks since my granny passed away and I find myself crying a lot. Even my Brother David has broken down in front of me and Claire. Claire had been right, that sooner or later, he would off-load all of his oppressed grief about our parents and it took loosing nana to do it. He cried in Claire's arms and asked for me to fetch the photo albums, he finally wanted to look through all the pictures of our parents, which nana was in so many of.

He opened up and started telling me and Claire so many different stories about mum and dad. He smiled as the memories came fresh to his mind. We all laughed out loud at one funny story he remembered, when our dad hadn't tied a bag down properly on top of the car roof. Whilst on a journey to Ireland, the bag had flown off and burst open somewhere in Wales and littered the road. Some of the clothes even landed on the cars that were travelling behind them. David explained how his dad looked so embarrassed as he stopped the car and made David help him gather up all of our mother's pieces of clothes, some of which were her underwear! David said our mother was holding me at the time and looked like she wanted the ground to just swallow her up. He recalled how they laughed all the way to catching the ferry at Holyhead afterwards.

It was really good to do this. It was a kind of healing for all of us that night. we went into our nana's room and all slept together in her, now giant, empty bed. She would have liked this. I knew that Fr. Marc (as I had started calling him) was beneath the bed and listening. He had fast become a real friend to me and is helping me through my loss. He has a way of explaining things to me, like no one else I have ever met, besides my nana.

18th of June 2014,
Dear Journal,

Things he told me, of times gone by, are beyond belief. I need to share this with someone, as I can't yet confide in my friends, not until Fr. Marc trusts them. I am dying to tell Kristian and for him to meet Fr. Marc, but until I can, I will share it all here with you, or with whoever may read this journal in the future.

So, this next part of my journal, is his story, Fr. Marcimus' and wow, what an incredible life story he has.

He was born in Italy, Venice, over a thousand years ago, the year was 975 AD. His father was a prison guard called Angelo and his mother had been a housemaid named Maria, sadly she died giving birth to him. Before she died, she named him Joseph James. His parents were not married, so he had been brought up by the Roman Catholic Church, where he learnt all about demons and angels. He never really had any real friends and spent most of his time reading. He was a quiet child and very well behaved.

His father would come to see him as often as he could, he longed for those days. His father would love to tell his son scary stories, which he would make up from the top of his head. He loved the way his father would add in real things that had happened at work in the prison, all sorts of bad characters, like murderers and dangerous thieves. Now and again, his father would make up stories about evil women called witches, who worshipped the Devil. They also spoke about their future and how someday soon, little Joseph James would be able to live with his father.

The year was 991 AD, Joseph was sixteen years old. He had grown up and was now a very handsome young man with jet black hair and the most piercing blue eyes. He was fit as a fiddle and so happy in life at that moment. With only two days to go before Joseph was due to leave the priests to go to live with his father (who had now married), for a second time in his short life, tragedy struck. His father had been at work inside the prison, he was walking a convict across the Bridge of Sighs, from the court house into the prison, when all of a sudden he started to choke. His face had turned red and no one could save him. In all the confusion the prisoner had got away, they think by jumping out of one of the many small windows and landing in the canal below.

Bit by bit, the story got out and Joseph heard many people's accounts of what had happened that day. The prisoner had been an old woman, who had murdered her own child, many years ago. She had never been caught, up until she tried to kill another child. Her name was Nula Black and people believed she was a witch and that she had poisoned poor Joseph's father. His job that day had been to take her across the bridge. People said it took a while for him to die and his eyes were pure black. Others said she was a child murderer and, wherever she had ever lived, children had gone missing. They believed she was responsible for at least eighty child deaths. A small army of men searched and searched, but no one ever saw her again, it's like she fell off the earth.

Joseph saw he only had one choice and that was to track this woman down and see justice for his father. With permission from the priests he went in search of her, all over Italy. After living rough for two years (the date was now 993 AD) and sleeping anywhere he could, he tracked her down deep in the woods outside of Rome. Nula Black lived in a wooden hut and was sleeping when he came across her. He tied her up whilst she slept and he then heard the cries of a newborn baby. She had stolen the baby boy from a young couple who had hired her to be their maid. Joseph was quick as lightning and got some local farmers to take the baby and reunite the little boy with his parents.

When he returned she was just waking up, so he threw holy water over her (he had, since a child, always carried some with him). She screamed as her face started to burn and huge, green blisters started to appear all over her face. He was so scared as she started to speak in several tongues. He suspected that she may try to put a curse on him, so to defend himself, in the only way he knew how, he started to pray. She went crazy and her body looked like it was being ripped from the inside, he heard her bones break and he just kept on praying, he didn't stop. When at last she lay still, he looked at her and what he saw was horrible, her eyes were jet black, like she had no soul.

Joseph told her who he was and asked her why she had to kill his father. Suddenly she let out a shriek of laughter and told him she would kill him next. He decided to throw more holy water over her and pray even harder. After five minutes he saw with his own eyes that she was possessed! The demon pulled itself from her body and looked him right in the eye, then in a flash was gone, at once he started to pray again. He prayed what his own father had taught him to say whenever he might feel scared; it was a special prayer to St. Michael the Archangel, he's the top angel in heaven, the very one who defeated the Devil for God and cast him out into hell.

Nula Black's body was free from the demon but it had claimed her life in the process. He gazed upon her face and she was an ugly woman, there was no denying that. Her hair was thin and grey, her skin was the worst he had ever seen in his life. He ventured back inside and looked around her home, dark magic was, without doubt, being practiced here. He found a book of spells and some other items that he would bring back with him to show the priests once he got home. He left her body there and informed the right authorities, which later came and dealt with the body.

Joseph became something of a hero and by the time he travelled back home, all in Venice had heard the tale of him, the witch and the baby he had saved. They welcomed him back with a big celebration. Once he got the chance to show the others what he had found in her den, it was clear to them, that she was a witch that became a willing host for the demon to live inside and commit evil crimes. They sent a letter and all the items to Rome for the Pope to see.

One month later Pope John XV sent for him. He packed up all his belongings and said goodbye to everyone in Venice who he knew; for the second time, but also, the last time in his life. Pope John XV had written, explaining that he needed him and had the perfect job waiting for him in Rome. He had to train to be a priest first and learn to speak many languages. He took the name Fr. Marcimus, because St Mark the Archangel was his favourite saint. It took many years to become the priest he needed to be, he studied hard and rose up through the ranks. While in Rome he saw the succession of five different Popes, who all passed on the secret mission from one to another. They all knew it was a much safer and wiser plan to keep his bound duty from the people, this was to stop any hysteria and false witch hunts that they all agreed was foreseeable. This would of course mean a very dark and dangerous future for many women who may arise suspicion or, in most cases, revenge but be totally innocent.

Then at the age of thirty, a whole twelve years later, he was deemed ready. His job was to be a witch and demon hunter This involved high risk to himself, there would be no doubt about the danger he would place himself in. He was fully trained to deal with any demonic cult, he had already, in Rome, performed over two hundred exorcisms (this is where the trained priest expels a demon from the body of its host using only prayers and holy water). Each time he performs an exorcism, he can, himself be at great risk of becoming possessed. The whole process leaves you so physically and mentally drained, it affects your health and emotional well-being.

It's the year 1005, the Pope now is called Pope John XVIII. Pope John XVIII himself declared him, Fr. Marcimus, to be his eyes in the battle between good and evil. The Pope revealed church secrets to him about an on-going battle between God and the Devil, a battle for our very souls. There was a war going on that the people of the world knew nothing about and he would be tested to the brink of madness. He must stay strong, the fate of the world and its billions of souls were relying on him.

He would leave Rome and travel the globe in search of any hint of black magic and witchcraft. He felt that with every witch he could catch, he was making his father proud in heaven. The next ten years saw him travel the world tracking down any inkling of those most foul of creatures. He spent three years in Africa and destroyed many voodoo witch doctors and was nearly killed in one village when he was poisoned by just a small child, who had offered him a drink of water. He had no idea that the child was in fact the village's own female witch doctor. She was very old, over a hundred he had been told, she was also very small and had sensed he was a priest. Her demon had warned her who he was and what he would do to her. By the grace of God, he escaped and got better by eating lots and lots of the honey he found.

From there, he sailed to Asia and explored that continent for just over three years, and again found many a witch there, where they loved to murder priests by fire. From there he decided to travel to the New World (America), where he reported back to Rome that there was an epidemic of witches. There, the witches were in great numbers, they had infiltrated the slave trade and the church. Whilst there he was attacked by one witch who stabbed him in the leg with a crystal shard. After that he ventured back to Europe where he helped to seek out over a hundred witches from nearly every city. He reported back to Rome that there was strong evidence that witches were seeking power - and in many cases gaining it. They were very clever and were holding many positions of power in palaces and castles all over the lands. They were becoming servants, nannies and maids, he even discovered plans of targeting all the kings in

Europe. Their plan was to attempt to become many a king's mistress or maybe, if they struck gold, even their wives, making them queens.

In 1012 he had become aware of dark powers at work in Rome, at it's very heart. He had to report back to Rome to meet the new Pope. This new Pope was called Pope Benedict VIII and he was sacred for his life. He explained in detail to Fr. Marcimus that evil was lurking at every turn, that even his own friends were against him, that he must watch his own back. He thanked Fr. Marcimus for all his hard service to God and for making the world a safer place.

He had yet another mission for him and, if he so wished, this could be his last task for Rome, as Fr. Marcimus was now forty years old. The assignment was to travel to England. There had now been too many reports coming back to Rome, that the Danish Vikings (who had for decades been raiding Anglo-Saxon England up and down the coast), were now, if it were to be believed, stealing their children by the hundreds. Vikings were known to take women and men for slaves and servants, sometimes, most of the time, they came to steal all the gold and money they could find, destroying villages and towns as they went. The pope explained that it just didn't add up that the Viking's were responsible for all of these stolen children. The question was, were Viking's snatching children? They invaded towns and villages and took what they wanted in loot and gold, but children?

The last Pope had sent good men to investigate. They had concluded that it was not the Vikings at all who were to blame, but that it was much more likely to be the coven of witches they had learnt about on their travels. Three witches in particular, who had fooled everyone into thinking they were sisters of good will. All three had come from Russia and were believed to be witches. They could fool many people and were trying hard to gain some power and influence. The Pope needed him to go and find out the truth, and if they were to be found stealing and killing children they needed to be burned alive. This, he told him, was to set a warning to all other women of ill will, that the church in Rome will not stand by and tolerate it anymore.

Joseph chose to go, but with the understanding that, once he captured and slayed the witches, he was free! Free from his duty and free from the priesthood. He had over the years dreamed of falling in love and being a father one day. Pope Benedict VIII agreed and promised him that he could leave the priesthood behind after this last mission. Looking into each other's eyes in deep thought, understanding what was at stake, they shook hands and became fast friends. He became at heart, very fond of this Pope and worried about his safety.

It only took Joseph two weeks to prepare for his final task. He had everything he might need and left Rome in the dead of night. He travelled by horse at first, then sold his horse to pay his way on a boat set for England. It was very cold in England and he wrapped himself up warm, it was a long and dangerous journey. Luckily for him he spoke English very well. He needed to decide where to start looking first, England was a big island after all and he needed all the information he could get by asking the right questions, to the right people. He found the English to be kind and hardworking, but very scared and fragile people. Always welcoming towards him, a priest, and helpful. He travelled far and wide across the land, seeking out any hint of witchcraft.

Over the years he had found a number of women who confessed to being part of a coven and many begged for mercy and claimed to have been used and brainwashed. Many of these women where telling the truth and so Fr . Marcimus blessed them and healed them of their misplaced judgement and loyalty. With the information he was given and the same three names he gathered, he was, each day, getting closer and closer to finding the three sisters. Each time one of the women confessed to him he learned a little more. Many of the women were punished with prison; he had, on his travels, come across lots of other stories of witches who had been killed by the local villagers because of fear. He was sure many of those women were most likely to have been innocent.

From the information he gathered, there was always the same three names that kept cropping up. These, he soon worked out, were the three sisters he had been searching for. They had managed to stay well hidden for a long time now. This told Fr. Marcimus that they had a network of witches and friends in high places who must be helping them out. No matter, he would track them down and he would, with God's power, cut them down and end their days of misery and darkness. The same would apply to anyone who was helping them.

Chapter 4
Gaining Power!

20th of June,
Dear Journal,

There doesn't seem to be enough hours in the day to hear all of Fr. Marcimus life story. I have wanted to sneak him into school with me, but we agree that it's too risky, so he stays home. He has enjoyed retelling his past, he reckons it's good for his brain and helps him remember things. He asks me lots of questions about my friends and spies on them when they come round before and after school. Over the past two days we have been doing a project on kings and queens - we are covering it together as a group. It has to be handed into our teacher in two days time, so having them come round is great, Fr. Marcimus can watch them and decide soon if he feels that we can trust them.

He sleeps in my room now in his little box beside my bed. My brother doesn't seem to mind at all that I have a newt as a pet, I can tell he just wants me to be happy and every now and again he will ask me if I am okay. At night, I listen to Fr. Marcimus' story - he just picks up from where he left off. Here is more of his tale and it really starts to get interesting.

After three years, he got a breakthrough and sent word to the Pope that he was closing in on the sisters, and he had heard that they were trying to gain influence on a noble lady, known today, as Ælfgifu of Northampton. I couldn't believe it when Fr. Marc explained that she was from the same area as me, although born over a thousand years ago. So that's why my nana came to Northampton all those years ago - she had chosen Northampton on purpose.

Fr. Marc explained that after he had been cursed and turned into a newt, he was first looked after by three little boys who had seen what happened and had helped him capture the three witches. He was passed on to sons and grandsons of each of those three boys over the years. Two of the boys' family lines died out when there were no more children, but one boy's family tree was still going strong and that was because his descendants had moved across the Irish sea to Ireland and took Fr. Marc with them.

They did this mainly because of the plague, the worst one in the history of the whole world (The Black Death). I remember learning about this in school, it was between the years 1346-53 AD. Historians estimate that between seventy-five to two hundred million people died. He told me it was a very scary time. He settled in Ireland, through the years he kept his eye on the news coming out of England, even so, over the years he began to forget about the Tree-Witches and tried very hard to live a normal life with whoever his companion was at the time. Of course he could never really forget, but there was really no point in worrying, until the one thousand years were up.

After he was passed over to my nana, they made plans together, to move to England. Nana stayed for many years, up until her mother became sick and she went back to take care of her. Fr. Marc went back with her as she had by then become his dearest friend. He explained to me that he had never had such a close bond with anyone else.

The truth was that in many ways he loved her. Their bond and love he told me was one of a kind. My nana was his soul mate and many times he wished that he could have changed back into a man, so that he could have married her, if she had wanted to. They would bare their souls to each other. My nana was the first girl ever that had been entrusted with him, before her it had always been a son or grandson that he and the secret were passed onto.

When he came back the first time with my nana, in the sixties, they were in fact searching for the very three trees that are the cursed Tree-Witches. They had no luck, Fr. Marc failed to remember the very spot where he had performed the curse. When he returned with my nana, after my parents car crash, They both tried to find them again and looked all over Northamptonshire. He just simply could not remember the name of the area. Plus, as it had been so many years ago, over time there were so many differences in the English language, it is more likely that the area has a different name now. Northampton and the midlands were known as Mercia a thousand years ago, he tells me.

I am so interested in all that he has to share with me, now that I am his companion. I hope I can help him when the time comes and that I don't let him down. I like to think that I am very brave but at the end of the day I'm just a young girl. Listening to him though is like having the very best history teacher you could ever wish for. Fr. Marc makes it all come to life and to know that he lived through it all is just crazy. One thing is for sure, I am so going to get an A+ in my history papers from now on - just think, I have a walking, talking answer book for history in my possession!

Speaking of history, back to Fr. Marc's story. The year, remember, is 1013 AD. This is when the witches started to gain some influence. They knew from their powers that there was a lady called Ælfgifu. She was destined to marry a future King of England (known today as Cnut the Great). He was to be the new young King of England (the ruler of England at the time was the Danish king, Swein Forkbeard). Cnut, his young son, was the head of his Danish army that conquered England.

To keep certain loyalties, King Swein had his young son Cnut married to Ælfgifu (joining of the hands as it was back then). So the Witches hatched a plan to gain her favour in the hope they would become handmaidens, If they succeeded, then who knew what power and influence they might gain? Their plan worked after they healed the lady Ælfgifu from morning sickness, with spells that they knew - they got positions within the court. A year later Cnut became King of England, due to his father's death.

Unfortunately for them, they soon showed their true colours. They hated the child she bore the King and plotted to have her and the child murdered. They plotted with others who at the time were against Cnut, mainly a man named Æthelred who had sent an army to force Cnut to flee back to Denmark, leaving his wife and baby son behind.

Thankfully for her, Svein, the future King of Norway, had both mother and child transported back safely to Denmark, along with the body of Cnut's father, King Swein (he had only been king for five weeks). She and her baby had escaped and those close to Cnut informed him of the witches treachery. They packed up, left and hid themselves away deep into one of the many forests, that covered most of Northamptonshire back in those times. Cnut's faithful servants found, in some of their belongings, some strange books, that in their panic, they must have unwittingly left behind them.

These books were of witchcraft and spells and one book in particular had in it, a list of all the children they had stolen over the years. At the time they were pretending to be kind, old women and promising to help them find their parents. The book named every last one of the poor little souls, it went into great detail of where and when the children were taken, from which area and how old they were, all were under ten years of age, some were under two and there was even a few babies taken.

Most of them were boys because they preferred boys. The most awful thing was the written account, of how the children were murdered. That's when I had to take a break and beg Fr. Marc not to go into any more detail. I didn't want to know how they died, it was bad enough knowing they had died, even if it was so long ago. Those poor children, I will pray for their souls and hope that they too are in heaven now and praying for mine. Fr. Marc told me that they would be. He sensed that they were in heaven with God and that they would for sure be praying for me, because they had known first-hand how evil and powerful those three witches were - and so would know what we were up against. That is, if we are to believe that there is any possible way those three evil witches can come back to life next year, when the thousand year old curse is lifted.

I have asked Fr. Marc about this, does he really believe that after all this time they could come back? He simply looked sad and told me that for many years he had asked himself why he was still here, why he was still alive and had been allowed to live so long, he could only assume that he is needed, that he has always had a greater purpose and that, is to finally defeat the witches. He must make sure he sends them to hell the very second the curse is lifted. That's why he has told me it is so important that we find those three trees - wherever they may be. I'm thinking to myself we had better hurry, as time is running out!

What will happen to the world if we never find the right trees - If we are too late and the curse is lifted, as Fr. Marc believes it will be? I ask myself how powerful could they possibly be after spending such a long time as trees.

Fr. Marc explained to me that they would be weak at first and in theory, easy to defeat there and then, but should they be allowed the time to heal and recover, then God only knows what will happen? They have, after all, demons inside of them and the devil can give them all the power they need to destroy this world. I pray for luck in finding those trees in time to destroy them. I pray for hope, we can only hope that good will always win over evil.

Chapter 5
The Bravest Boys!

3rd of July 2014
Dear Journal,

After sometime, I got to thinking about the three little boys that Fr. Marc had told me briefly about. So, as soon as I got the chance, I thought I would ask him more about them. One day, while we were alone and walking in a wood near to my village, I did.

"Fr. Marc please tell me all about the three young boys who helped you catch The Tree-Witches, like what were there names? How old were they?".

"I suppose I should, yes, seeing as you descend from one of those wee lads".

"What were their names?"

"Leo, Matthew and Noah,"

"which one am I descended from?" I asked.

"Leo, he was the little leader of the group, I remember well, like it was yesterday."

Fr. Marc had a peculiar look on his face as he started to remember them all. I could tell he had been very fond of them. That gave me the idea that I should write their story down and add it to my journal. The next part is their story and this is what Fr. Marc told me about what happened as best as he could remember - after all he is over a thousand years old!

Fr. Marc was hot on the trail of the three sister's. He knew that there could only be a few villages between him and them. They were using the land that belonged to the lady Ælfgifu, who was of course the land owner of these parts. They must have been hiding somewhere close by and most likely in the woods and forests that were scattered everywhere.

He had got word from Rome that the Pope had recently had to flee Rome for his life. The threat was very real and came from Gregory VI who opposed him as Pope. He had compelled Pope Benedict VIII to leave and became an antipope in his place. These were dark times for the church. He prayed his friend Pope Benedict would find safety and protection from his enemies where ever he might be. Marc must carry out his own mission and was heading for another village close to where Kirah's many plus times great grandfather Leo was living and his cousins Matthew and Noah. This is the part they played.

The three boys were all first cousins and came from the same village, they were just 10 years old at the time. Leo was the kind of 'take charge lad who liked to take his cousins under his wing and go on adventures with them or go exploring. He had curly blonde hair and big blue eyes. He was powerfully built and as quick as a hare. Their village had been attacked a few times by Vikings so the three lads knew how to look after each other and use weapons such as knives and swords. Their father's taught them well and they were often called to go hunting for the village as they had shown great talent for capturing game (like deer and rabbit).

Matthew was the kindest and was ever so gentle. All the children in the village loved for him to play with them. He also had blonde hair and blue eyes. His hair was kept as short as possible.

Noah the youngest cousin was very tall for his age and had long wavy hair which was also blonde and he had the most amazing deep green eyes. Noah being very strong and always wanting to help mend things was sort after. Not just his parents but people from all around would often ask him for his help. He was just so talented with his hands, a true carpenter.

Noah had just been helping fix some wooden posts when he heard the news. He travelled back from visiting his uncles village as quick as he could. He brought the news back with him that there was a lone priest hunting three women in the area. Three odd looking women who were responsible for many children's disappearance. The news had spread from village to village that he believed them to be witches and was asking if anyone had seen or heard of these women.

People were very worried for their own little ones and agreed to help the priest in any way they could. Noah told Leo and Matthew that every man in his uncles village joined with the men from the next village and went in a great mass to search the woods all around them. Then, suddenly, he said there was great panic as one of the women started howling and screaming saying a demon had taken her child, a little girl aged five called Annabelle.

Noah wanted to help search for her too but his father insisted that he hurry back home and warn their village. He wanted all the men of his village to join in the search for these witches and burn them alive. Then they would come home heroes and there would have to be a joining of all the village's to celebrate their deaths. Fr. Marc, the priest, would be their special guest. Noah's mother, along with other women in the village, were to prepare a wonderful banquet for the priest and villagers.

The three boys watched as the news spread around the village, all the men started to leave and the women were running around like headless chickens. The boys could hear their own mother's calling them and knew that they would be expected to help gather the crops to cook, help skin some rabbit, and gather lots and lots of water. That's when Leo gets an idea!

"Why should we stay here and help the women, when we could be out there, looking for the witches who must have taken that girl? I say we should go help our mothers for a wee bit, then meet back here in, say, half an hour, and then go ourselves. What do you say cousins, nobody knows these woods better than us?"

"You're right cousin Leo, and if we are the ones to catch the witches and save the little girl, then we will become the heroes! You with us cousin Matthew?"

"Yes, let's do this. I'll go and get my weapons and take some of the holy water my mother recently got on her way back from church. It will help, witches hate anything holy don't they?"

"Great idea cousin Matthew, cousin Noah you go look for some too and bring back with you any crosses that you can find."

So, while their mothers were busy cooking and preparing the village for the celebration, the three boys sneaked away past them. Their village was the biggest in the area at that time. They were heading in one direction for the Northern Wood, close by, when suddenly Matthew spotted a cloaked woman the other side of the village, that brought alarm bells to him. A little baby, about a year old, looked as though she was sleep-crawling towards her. He watched a second more and sensed something was not right.

The hairs stood up on his arms, why wasn't that woman helping the other women? He pointed it out to his two cousins and they stopped and watched too. They realized the woman was controlling the little baby and leading her away from the village. They watched how the woman, in a flash, swung the baby girl up into her arms and away she ran into the dusk. She was heading to the south and towards the forest there. This was known to be the largest forest by far in these parts and you could keep yourself well hidden for weeks if you wanted to. It was all adding up to the boys, so they watched and followed without the witches knowledge.

She led them deep into the forest, she still had a firm hold of the baby girl who was not screaming and so must have still been under some kind of spell. They watched as the witch met up with another woman. The boys figured that she too must be one of the three witches the priest was searching for. She was wearing a hooded cloak also, this made it hard for the boys to see their faces. But they could see that she had with her a little girl. The boys quickly worked out that it must be the same child called Annabelle, stolen from Noah's uncle's village. Yes, Noah recognised her. They stayed back and well hidden behind some bramble brushes. They watched and waited and then carefully followed them through some thick thorn bushes that seemed to go on forever. On the other side, they could see there was a wooden cabin and watched as the two witches hurried inside. They had to come up with a plan to trap the three witches and then kill them before any harm came to the children. They stayed well back and hidden from sight, as they hatched a plan.

"I have an idea, you know, not far from here is the old well, that we sometimes use to refresh ourselves when out hunting for hours."

"You're right! What you want to do cousin, trap them down there?"

"No cousin Matthew, listen, that would be too hard and afterwards we would have to lift them out to burn them, it wouldn't be safe. They must know that it's here, even witches have to drink sometimes and they need water to cook with."

"Come on, tell us cousin, what plan have you come up with?"

"We are going to tip all our holy water into that well and pray they come out soon to gather some water, then sit back and watch, it won't be long before they are running scared and screaming or howling from their cabin."

"Do you really think it will work? I mean me and Matthew always wonder, does holy water have any real power?"

"Holy water cured my dad once remember, of course it will work, and we shall keep a little bit on us too and have a cross each to protect us."

"I will go round the front of the cabin and keep watch, you both go at the back and see if you can see anything. Try and get close enough to a window to throw one of the crosses in, place another one at the back door."

They quickly got into position once they heard loud crying and the baby screaming. Suddenly, just as Leo had predicted, one of the witches came out of the front of the cabin. She had with her a huge drum and ventured over to the well. She was wearing a black hooded cloak which was covering her face. Leo watched her. She was really a big size, so fat, and then he saw her lower her hood. Seeing her face, which was so ugly and pig-like, made him feel physically sick. She started leaning over the well, trying to reach the bucket. He could see she was reaching far over the well. He suddenly thought that maybe he should push one of them in and be done with it, with any luck she would die on the way down. This would make it easier on them, it wouldn't be three against three anymore, but three against two.

The next thing he knew he was rushing towards her and before she could react it was too late. He pushed her over with all his might and down she fell into the well. The only thing left of her, was her black hooded cloak that had got caught in Leo's hunting knife. She had been so taken by surprise, that she didn't even make a sound. Leo looked down and saw the bucket was nearly up and was half full of water. He couldn't see any sign of her and so turned around and whistled to his cousins.

Chapter 6
The Rescue!

5th of July 2014
Dear Journal,

Listening to Fr. Marc recall this event from so far back in his past, has me captivated. The hours that pass by, feel like only minutes to me. I can't wait to get in from school to hear more of this story. I always get comfortable in the den, in my favourite corner. I always bring an apple with me for a snack. Once I settle down, Fr. Marc will begin where he left off. For me it feels like I'm actually there, I can picture it all in my mind, how the boys looked and must have felt and I imagine how creepy it must have been in those woods. Back to the story we go:

Both Matthew and Noah knew what this meant when they heard it - Leo's whistling, as it was one of their hunting whistles to warn each other of wolves and bears in the area (safety in numbers), so they ran back over to meet up with him and found him wearing one of the witches cloaks.

"what happened cousin? How did you gain this?" Noah pointed at the cloak.

"Listen fast cousins we have little time, I used your idea Noah and pushed one of them down the well, it was just too tempting and it will make it easier to catch the other two, now that it's three against two. She didn't scream and that is strange, I think maybe she is stuck half way down, she was so terribly fat!"

"What shall we do now cousin Leo?" "First, just in case she is trying to climb back up, help me place this large rock across the well to keep her well and truly trapped."

The three cousins lifted a very heavy rock. Once in place on the well, all three turned towards the cabin. They could now hear the other two witches complaining as to why she was taking so long. They were complaining that she was too slow and lazy. Her greediness was becoming a problem.

"With this cloak over all three of us" Leo explained "we will look big enough to fool them into thinking that we are her, just long enough to throw this holy water in their faces from the bucket. We need to walk in backwards, as not to give ourselves away."

"Great idea Cousin Leo."

"Cousin Matthew, you hold the bucket and once I yell NOW! I want you to release the holy water all over them, it's down to you cousin to get this right."

"what shall I do?" Asks Noah.

"Our job cousin, is to find the baby and girl and get them out of there as quickly as we can and place them somewhere safe."

Little did the boys know, that an alarm had been raised in their village over their disappearance and that of the little baby, named Beth. Their three fathers had come running back and with Beth's father had demanded every man to search for them.

They begged Fr. Marc to come with them. He agreed and seemed to sense the witches were getting desperate. They must be taking these silly risks because they need young souls. Young, pure souls to steal and devour to keep their strength up. Fr. Marc had God on his side and something was telling him to go into the biggest forest on the southern side of the village. The four father's agreed and off they marched.

Meanwhile Leo, Noah and Matthew were all cloaked over and heading towards the blood stained wooden cabin. All three of them could feel their hearts racing and hear them pumping. They had never been so scared before in their short lives, but they were determined to be just as brave (by God they were).

Once inside the door, a smell hit them like they couldn't believe. It was worse than rotting meat or fish. That's one of the signs, that what you're dealing with, is pure evil and demonic. It brought tears to the young boys' eyes and through their blurry vision they scanned the room.

They could see the two witches hunched over their cauldron. Their eyes darted about and finally spotted the little girl, Annabelle, who had been left holding the baby, Beth. Annabelle looking so frightened and sick, too scared, even to move or run away. The terror in their eyes made the cousins so angry they quickly set to work and lashed out their very own punishment.

"NOW! MATTHEW NOW!" Shouted Leo and Noah and on cue, just at the right moment. Matthew had timed it perfectly, as with one huge toss, he managed to hit both witches right in their faces, just as they turned around in shock to confront all the yelling.

"Quick take the girls!" Screamed Leo to Noah. Noah who was very strong, just bounced into action and lifted them both up together. Before either of the witches could react he ran out of the cabin, into the dark forest for safety. Annabelle was still holding baby Beth in her small arms. Noah hid well away, but could still see the dirty little cabin, with its horrible, yellow, glowing window. He said a silent prayer for his friends, that they would make it out of there alive and go back to the village with him, as heroes.

"AWRRRRRRRRRRHHHH!!!!! You will pay for this, we will skin you alive". Screamed one of the witches.

The holy water worked. Leo and Matthew watched as, the ugliest of any creatures they had ever landed their eyes on, melted. Their faces started turning green, huge blisters popping on their cheeks. There were big, yellow, puss-pockets bursting yellow ooze down their faces. One of the witches face's was hit harder and was covered the most in holy water. She screamed and screamed, holding her hands up to her face, trying to hold her falling-apart face together. The other, older witch, didn't make a sound, she didn't take her eyes off them. She seemed to be smiling and was coping quite well for someone whose face was falling off. The oldest witch snarled at them.

"Where's our sister, you little rats, what have you done with her? You don't know who you're dealing with , we will make you wish you had never been born."

"We will never tell you and we are not sacred of you. We know that you are WITCHES!" Said Leo.

"Come sister, let's teach these boys a lesson they will never forget and make it as painful as ours." Hissed the same witch.

The other witch slowly looked up and half her face, which they hadn't noticed before, was indeed extremely beautiful and the other half was being destroyed by the holy water that had just been thrown over her.

"I want to kill this one Dragoona. You must let me have him. He threw the poison, he is to blame, the one who has stolen my beauty, HOW I WILL MAKE HIM SUFFER." She roared.

"HUSH! Serpentina, don't you worry. You may have him and do what you will with him, but first, we must make them tell us where our sister Hogonna is."

"Yes, you're right of course sister and we must find that other pest who stole our children."

Hearing her use the words 'our children', made Leo so furious, he lashed out.

"They're not your children, you evil, ugly witches. We will never tell you where our cousin is or for that matter where your greedy hideous sister is!"

"Then you die boy. You and your friends. We will skin you alive one by one - and you will go last, so you can have the pleasure of watching the others and hearing their last screams."

Both witches made a dash for a boy each. Dragoona aimed for Leo and Serpentina for Matthew. For old women they sure could move fast and both were able to grab the boys before they could run.

They were unbelievably strong and lifted both boys up into the air. The two witches snarled in the boys' faces and the boys could see their rotting teeth (of which there were not many). Their breath was so fowl it brought tears to the boys' eyes. But, by far the worst thing, was their eyes - jet black, full of hate and darkness, demon eyes.

They both started to laugh as they moved back across the room towards the lit fire. The plan, was to torture the boys, before killing them. The room was full of cages, some on the floor, most hanging from the ceiling. In some of them, the boys could see small bones and some old clothes that must have once belonged to some children. Both boys could still smell the putrid air that was all around them.

The witches grabbed hold of a boy each. Leo looked at his smaller cousin and shouted to him "JESUS", and just like that, both boys got their crosses and, with all the strength they had left, they rammed the crosses into the witches foreheads. The crosses burned into their very flesh. Both witches screamed and dropped the boys to the blood soaked floor. They had raised both their hands to their decaying and now burning faces. Their dirty long sharp fingernails had yellow puss running down them, as there were now, huge blister's exploding out, on their faces.

The boys didn't wait. As soon as the witches lost their grip on them, the boys were gone. They ran from that cabin as fast as they could, very nearly falling over themselves. They were so scared, their feet didn't seem to be working properly. They called and whistled out for their cousin Noah, praying he was safe and hoping he would answer them. In their panic they kept running in circles, they both heard wings gush by their heads. They soon felt some birds pecking their faces as they ran. They were under attack by huge crows.

They fell to the ground and then, after what seemed an age, got up and ran straight into the witches. These were remember, no ordinary witches, but demonic ones. With their black magic they could transform themselves into crows. They had cleverly trapped the boys where they wanted. With great speed they had transformed back into human form.

It was very dark in the wood now and the moon above gave little light to those below. In fact the moon looked as though it was turning red. The witches dragged Leo and Noah with ease. Dread started to arise in Leo's chest, as he recognised that they were heading towards the well, not the cabin.

They arrive at the well and the witches spotted the rock in place and smiled at one another.

"Well well, you boys have been busy!"

The witch called Dragoona effortlessly knocked off the rock. Out flew something big and landed in front of them all.

"Sister Hogonna so glad you could join us, we have been searching for you."

"They pushed me down the well. I want to eat every last one of them."

Hogonna looked so crazy, that her big chubby head, appeared as though it was about to explode.

"Well you must learn to wait your turn. I am in charge, and for now they are mine and I say, we throw them down the well! You agree sister? Let's see how they like it. We sisters can play a game of hide and forget ever after! They can starve down there."

Both Hogonna and Serpentina looked creast fallen, as they just wanted so badly to rip into the boys, spill all their guts out and be done with them. But they knew that Dragoona loved to play games with her prey, before she went in for the kill.

"Then after that, can we pull their teeth out? It will be so painful for them and we can drown in the pleasure of their screams." Dragoona continued.

Chapter 7
The Escape!

7th of July 2014
Dear Journal,

Today my brother David nearly caught me talking with Fr. Marc. He popped his head into the den, because he was starting to get a bit worried about me, because of all the time I seem to spend in there. He could hear voices and listened for a while and then was shocked to find me alone. I had to act fast and tell him that I was rehearsing for a role that I want to do at school for the drama club. He told me that he thought that was great. He declared that I would get picked for sure, as he never heard anyone in his life talk so much and in different accents. Once David left Fr. Marc was able to continue the story:

Noah had been waiting and watching. He was keeping the girls warm, wrapped up in his arms. He saw his cousins flee from the cabin and then he saw the witches chase after his cousins. He watched as the three witches turned into birds, black birds like crows. He couldn't believe his eyes. He could feel the sweat of fear start to trickle down the side of his face. He wished he could escape the sounds that the three crows were making together as they circled above the heads of his cousins. The forest had become so dark now and the boys were running around in circles. He heard them call out his name, he wanted so much to warn them.

God, how he wished he could warn them of just how deadly, powerful these witches were. But there was no way of calling out or whistling to them, without giving away were he and the girls were hiding. He had found an old, fallen tree which was covered in ivy, for them to stay hidden in. The tree had rotted over time and now it had become hollow in the middle. The space was just big enough for all of them to squeeze into and stay out of view. The wood was so very dark and he could hardly see. He felt all around him, how damp the hollow tree was, and he could smell his own fear.

He looked down into the innocent faces relying on him, to save them. Their frightened eyes shining out of the darkness, was all he could see and think about. He had got them to stop crying and they trusted him now. He could see it in their little eyes, the hope. His job now was to protect them, he had to get them out of there before the witches found them. He just would have to hope that his cousins would be able to out run the witches. He prayed that they would find a way out.

He decided he had to make his move and so gathered the girls and moved silently away, until his cousin's cries, for him, were silent. It wasn't long before he could smell wood burning. He could see balls of flames up ahead, floating back and forwards. Help had come, so he ran as fast as he could with the two little girls clinging onto him. He didn't stop, until he ran straight into the group of men holding their torch of fire in one hand and their sword in the other. All had a look of fear on their faces - they were wise to be so frightened. Once the fathers of the little girls saw them, they ran, they took their daughters from him into their arms, kissing the top of their heads. Annabelle's father turned to speak to Noah.

"Bless you boy for returning our daughters safe to us; we will never be able to repay you."

Both men quickly turned around and headed back to their village to take their daughters home and into the comforting arms of their mothers. At the same time, a big man, who was Noah's father, along with Fr. Marcimus, started to push his way hurriedly through to the front.

"Noah my son, thank God you're safe!"

"Father, quick, cousins Leo and Matthew are in great danger! We found the witches lair. I escaped with the girls they had stolen. I fear for them father, it's so dark in the forest now. They were running so hard but in their panic kept turning the wrong way and the witches were close by. I couldn't warn them father, I wanted to, but I had to keep the girls safe. I'm sorry father, uncles, please forgive me for leaving them behind and abandoning them."

Noah couldn't help but have tears in his eyes as he spoke, he was trying his hardest not to cry. All the men knew just how close these three young boys were. Over the years they had seen them grow up together and play together. They were thinking of the times that the boys would tease the girls of the village. Some of the girls being daughters of the men here in the gathering. They all knew and had seen how much they had grown and what a fine hunting team they were. They could hear the love for his cousins in his voice as he tried to hold it together.

Noah's father took his son by the shoulders and looked up to the men. He glanced around him and he could see that his son's words had brought lumps to the men's throats. He looked at his own brothers and saw tears in their eyes, tears of love. They were all remembering their own childhood, it brought it all back. Like the three cousins, there was nothing that they wouldn't do for each other. Noah's two uncles came and stood by him and each placed a hand on his shoulder. All three brothers looked into each other's eyes. Confirming that they knew, that their three sons, were boys no longer! That they would come out of that forest as young men.

Fr. Marcimus came forward, as he could see and feel all the emotions in the men around him. This was good, there was so much love there among those men. Most were brothers, fathers and sons. They would stop at nothing until their village and their families were all safe.

"Noah, I am Fr. Marcimus and I need you to listen to me. You boys were very brave and I need you to keep being brave. We need you now to lead us back into the forest and help us find those evil witches and to save your cousins and all mankind."

"Yes, I'm ready to fight. I can show you the way. Let's hurry as the witches could have them by now! Fr. Marcimus I think you had better be aware that these women are not just some ordinary witches, they have dark magical powers. I saw them turn themselves into crows, Father"

Back at the well the witches took turns to beat the two boys black and blue. The blows that were rained down on them, were not the normal force of ordinary women, such as their own mothers who had once or twice beaten their sons for being disobedient. These women possessed a dark power, and it was strong. All Leo and Matthew could do, was hold onto each other and hope they didn't lose consciousness. The grip on each other's arms gave them the strength to hang in there for one another. The witches were enjoying the beating and were preparing to lift both lads up and toss them into the well where they would then simply cover it up and leave them there to die.

Both Leo and Matthew gave each other a look in the darkness of the forest. It was a look of love, regret and goodbyes. They were just boys. only ten years old, how could this be the end they both wondered? But they were joint in their happiness, that their cousin Noah, the youngest of them, had got away and saved the little girls. Suddenly Leo had an idea!

"Praise the lord for saving cousin Noah and the children. Our sacrifice is worthy in the eyes of God. He will not desert us as we face death. We do not fear death knowing we will be heroes in heaven." He smiled across at Matthew.

"Yes God is the almighty one and He will always triumph over evil." Matthew added.

All three witches suddenly stopped and threw the two boys down hard onto the ground. Their faces twisted with hate and rage, as they reacted to what they heard the boys say. This had been the boys' plan, to distract the witches from what they were doing. The oldest of the witches took the lead and began to reply in a hiss like voice - a snake like hiss!

"Your God is a cowardly God and all who believe in him are fools. He will never win this war, as there will always be more like us everywhere you turn. You useless, stupid boys, your God doesn't care about you, He simply watches and does nothing, because he's weak. He has turned his back, He has given up on His poor creation, MAN! There are upon millions and millions of us. You weaklings could never imagine the power we possess. A power given to us by Satan himself and we will help him capture every last one of your souls and drag you all into hell."

"YOU LIE!" Shouted out a voice full of hope and confidence.

Leo and Matthew, as well as the witches, turned around in surprise to face a small army of men, with Noah in the middle, standing beside what looked like a monk. This man had the purest of blue eyes and he held a cross of Christ in his hand, with such belief and assurance. Both Matthew and Leo thanked God that their prayers had been answered. Both boys looked at one another and took the opportunity of the witches distraction to kick them as hard as they possibly could in the shins and then run away. The witches failed to stop them and once they joined Noah, all three boys embraced one another and smiled. They had lived to tell the tale, they would be sung heroes by tonight back in their village.

Inside their minds, the boys were picturing their village party - the wonderful food and fuss which would be made over them. The younger boys in the village would look up to them like they were heroes and all the girls would be smiling at them and wanting to do everything for them. They were so lucky to be alive, not every child meets a witch (in their case three), and lives to tell the tale.

Chapter 8
Death to the Witches!

7th of July 2014
Dear Journal,

I have not been able to concentrate today at school. I got told off for day dreaming about a million times. Those teachers haven't a clue about what I'm going through. Imagine a world of witches, you're there, you're re-living it and all you want to do is get home and hear the rest of the story. I barge my way into the house so quick, that I nearly knock poor Claire over. She wants to know what my hurry is, I make up some lie about meeting Kristian.

Then I straight away regret it, as I see the smile she gives me and then she winks. Oh dear Lord the shame of it - now she thinks I have a crush on Kristian! Well I kind of do, but she doesn't need to know that. Oh God help me, if she tattles to my brother, he will never leave me alone. I decide to just find Fr. Marc, to put my mind at rest, as he continues the tale.

The witches were totally taken by surprise, they were quickly surrounded by all the men. They tried in vain to escape by fighting back, even managing to hurl a good ten of the men into the air - as if they were babies; but there were just too many men for them to deal with. The men pounced on the witches - one man after another; why the witches didn't turn themselves back into crows they didn't know. They didn't care just as long as they were captured.

Maybe they could only use that spell once? Very quickly they tied the witches up with the blessed robe Fr. Marc had given them. Fr. Marc gave them instructions to lead them out of the forest and back towards the village. All the men got quickly to work, gathering all the firewood they could muster. Leo and Matthew embraced their cousin Noah and then set to work too.

Once the three mounds of wood were high enough, each witch was placed on one, with their hands tied to a wooden pole behind them.
There was to be no escape for them this time. Fr. Marc had his bible in his hand and looked up at the three witches. He could see no fear in any of their eyes and this worried him. He knew he had to stay strong and brave. He knew that their power was strong as soon as he had come in contact with the three witches - it was reaching out and pulling at his mind. Their

power was different from all the other witches that he had ever encountered.

These women, he knew, had fully welcomed a demon each. Demons from hell to possess their bodies. They had totally given into the demons. There was nothing left of the women they once were, he did not doubt, but he must still try and reach whatever remaining part of them he could. His job was to destroy these witches, he knew that and, to show them no mercy. The way of the church is to always give a choice of confessing sins. It was for some kind of redemption if they wanted it - it would always remain, at the end of the day, between them and God.

"Hear me you wretched beings, I know you are servants of the devil. I know you willingly sold your souls to Satan for the power he gave you. Where is he now as you're about to come face to face with your maker?" He yelled.

"I know who you are, you demon witches, with crimes of old! Your names will never be forgotten. You, Hogonna, who loves to devour little children. You, Serpentina, who likes to trick men and rip off their flesh. Lastly Dragoona, name of the beast, you claim to be three sisters, this is a lie. You hate with all your will. You are the queens of hell, and you will rot there once I'm through with you." He looked for a reaction. "The one true God will prevail. You will burn to death and you will burn in hell, But if you were to renounce Satan now, for all his empty promise's and beg God for forgiveness, then who knows but God, that your pitiful souls may be saved from the flames of hell."

Fr. Marc looked up at all three witches, the fat one and the youngest had their eyes closed, as if they were asleep, but the one named Dragoona, the leader, was smiling from ear to ear. This unnerved Fr. Marc just a little, as he waited for their reply. Seconds passed by and they felt like hours. Their time was up and as he took a lightened torch and set the wood ablaze he heard the laughter of the demons. The mound of wood below her would not light! He ran to another mound beside her to the left with Serpentina above it and that wouldn't light either.

He started to sweat as he ran back to the sounds of their combined laughter and tried, in vain, to set fire to the witch, Hogonna. Again he failed and whilst fretting, he decides he must get as many men as possible, with torches, to help him light the wood. He could feel every pair of eyes on him. All the villagers and their children were there too, watching him. He must not fail.

He could feel Dragoona, with her wild and waving, dark, blue hair, watching him and latching onto his innermost thoughts of failing. He looked into the eyes of the devil himself and knew that, no matter how he was tested, he would see this through to the bitter end.

"SET FIRE TO THEIR CLOTHES!" Fr. Marc roared at the top of his voice.

"YOU WILL ALL DIE THIS NIGHT FOR THERE IS NO POWER GREATER THEN THAT GIVEN TO US." Roared Dragoona.

Each man tried, but it was futile, the witches just would not burn and people started to panic. Fr. Marc demanded calm and order.

"We shall drown them instead." He declared.

Everyone thought this was a great idea. After getting the witches down, they led them to the river. Once at the riverbank, some of the men helped walk the witches deep into the water. The witches hands were still tied together.

Fr. Marc couldn't help but start to feel a little uneasy, sweat was starting to run down his face from his forehead. Locking eyes with Dragoona, Fr. Marc noticed that she wore, again, the same cruel smile pursed on her blood red lips. He had an awful foreboding that this wasn't going to work either. He was right. It didn't matter that they had their hands tied, the witches didn't drown.

Getting desperate, Fr. Marc asked some men to hold them down under the water - even this tactic wouldn't work. It didn't seem to matter how long they were held under the water; each time they came back up they laughed into the night. The villagers were becoming scared and the men in the water were getting cold; soon it would be dawn.

"HANG THEM!" Cried out one of the women.

Fr. Marc couldn't think of what to do next and so, he agreed. They soon dragged the witches out of the river and found that close by was the perfect tree. One of the villagers, with a rope tied to his back, climbed up the tree. He quickly tied it into position with a noose at one end. He repeated this twice more, further along the thick branch of the tree. Another man had brought back three horses and, together, with his fellow neighbours, managed to get all three witches astride a horse each.

"Now, listen to me, you most evil of women. You must pay for what you did, the pure innocence that you stole and murdered. We will show you no mercy, you will have to hope, you can find some with God. Place on their nooses." Called Fr. Marc.

"You pathetic little excuse for a priest, you still don't understand who you are dealing with do you?" Hissed Dragoona.

Then, with her sisters, she started laughing and screaming. This frightened the horses and without needing to be slapped, each horse just suddenly bolted. The horses could sense the evil upon their backs and ran away. Everyone watched, as in slow motion, the nooses tightened around their necks. They were left hanging in the air for only a spit second, as all three of the witches ropes snapped. They landed like experts on their feet and stood up straight glaring with defiance at everyone around them. They each had a crazy look in their eyes, which were ablaze with a different colour from the others. Dragoona's eyes were a flaming red, Serpentina's eyes were the serpent yellow of a Cobra, as for Hogonna, hers were purple and glowing. Suddenly the rope which had tied their hands together snapped as well.

Fr. Marc saw the alarm and horror on everyone's faces. The first to run away were all the women with their little ones. Their panicking feet lifting up the dust on the ground.

"We have had enough of these silly, feeble games of yours. Now, little priest, it's our turn to have fun and by Satan's fire, we are going to rip you all apart, one by one and eat your souls. Where is your God now PRIEST!" She spat out.

Fr. Marc saw most of the men now turn and run away. He could feel some kind of battle rage inside his own mind. Where was his God? Why wasn't he protecting the people and him? How could he expect him to defeat this kind of evil all on his own? Then he saw the three boys Leo, Matthew and Noah standing right behind him and with them, were their fathers and what must have been other close family members and friends. They believed in him; he could use their faith right now, he needed it. The look of absolute trust in all of their eyes, they were loyal to the end. They would not abandon him, their eyes told him so. He suddenly thought of God and knew that He hadn't deserted him. He had sent him all the help he could ever need - man's pure faith in goodness and how it will always prevail over evil. He must do something and then he wondered, why on earth hadn't he thought of it before? In his panic to kill the three witches he forgot to perform an exorcism on the witches.

This was a vital mistake on his part. He was so mad with himself, how could he have forgotten. All along God had given him the power. He had the power before he even landed in this country, for some strange reason, he just chose to forget it. He was an expert exorcist. He had to do this, to banish the evil spirits and send them back to where they had come from - hell itself. Then he would destroy the witches.

He knew there and then, that ever since he met them, they had been playing games with him. They had read his mind, seen his weakness or most likely the demons inside them had made them aware. So he had, himself, been manipulated by them, sidetracked - and they were enjoying every minute of the show. They were toying with him.... well not for much longer.

Chapter 9
The Curse!

8th of July 2014
Dear Journal,

Poor Fr. Marc has nearly lost his voice with all the talking he has been doing of late. He secretly loves hot chocolate and I made him one to cheer him up and, as he enjoys his full mug, in little whispers, he carries on where he left off, the story of the Tree-Witches. He's just a wonderful story teller and I can't wait to hear the final piece of what happened on that day a thousand years ago.

It has only just gone past midnight, but with the rain hitting hard at the window and all this new information running around in my head, I can't sleep. Fr. Marc is peacefully asleep now. He looks as cute as a button in his box. I made him carry on telling me everything about his tale until the end. I shall share it with you now, as I am starting to feel so tired and drained by it all.

He was very cold, so he pulled from his chest pocket his trusty bible, which was so worn and torn looking. He placed it to his lips and kissed it, as if greeting an old friend. He spoke in

Latin and read from the pages out loud and then started the ritual. The words rolled off his tongue as he knew so much of it off by heart. He knew now that he had their attention, as all three witches started to struggle.

Their bodies seemed to be giving up the fight, but they still had their tongues and by God, did they use them! Each taking it in turn to scream out threats and swear words. Fr. Marc could always hear the demons in their voices and smell the foulness of them, ever since he first came across the witches. He could now see for sure the demons in their menacing faces and sinister eyes. They had latched onto these women like ticks on dogs and wouldn't give up, not without a fight. He brought out his small bottle of holy water. He then threw some on them while repeating the Latin prayers. The demons were getting no rest but they still could be a threat as there was nothing holding them back from attacking him and ripping him apart.

They sensed this and made their move as Fr. Marc slowly trod backwards. He needed to stay focused and keep praying till he could force the demons out of their bodies. He didn't see the rock behind him in time to avoid it. He went crashing heavily to the ground, he hurt his back in the fall. They were ready to pounce on him and devour his flesh. He could see the hunger for his soul in their eyes. They crept closer and were about to consume him, when the boys and their fathers ran, aiming their swords at the witches hearts. He managed to crawl back a yard or two. This of course didn't slow them down for long as the demon witches cut through the swords like butter.

Fr. Marc wished for strength and a miracle. He was just so tired now, he had a feeling of hopelessness about him and failure. He was letting them get to him, invading his mind. He had very little energy left and wished he could just hold them off a while longer. A thousand years, say, would do it, he wished for himself. He could be all rested and relaxed - like one of those trees over there, minding his own business, before he had to face these demon witches again.

He looked up as he could hear Dragoona recanting a spell towards him. All sorts of nightmarish thoughts raced through his mind. He didn't want to make eye contact with her anymore, but he couldn't help but stare into her eyes. They were the deadest eyes he had ever encountered, so cold and evil, so beast-like. He tried to concentrate; what kind of spell was she going to place on him? He couldn't help but wonder. Maybe turn him into some kind of reptile that he hated, like a frog or lizard, and then eat him in one gulp. He sent up one final prayer, out loud, to his God.

"Please help me Lord, now is the time to show your greatness and power. Help me to defeat these demon witches."

A flash of lightening and a horrible roar of thunder, as if the whole planet was breaking in two, was all he could remember, just before the witches reached him. Next thing he knew, it was pouring with rain and he just lay there in the mud. The three witches, who were just a few feet away from him, stopped as if their own feet were rooted to the ground. The next few moments were like a dream; Fr. Marc, it seemed to him, was getting smaller as the witches were getting bigger, as they grew though they seemed to stretch out. It seemed that they never moved from their spot on the ground.

God had shown his power alright and like straight out of a children's tale, something mysterious started to happen to the witches. Fr. Marc could not believe his eyes as the witches started to turn into trees. He enjoyed the fear in their eyes. First their toes burst from their shoes and began to turn into what looked like the white thick roots of trees that grow underground. They were screaming and wailing like the Banshee of Ireland, for he had heard it once, long ago.

Fr Marc could still see the demons behind the eyes of the witches and laughed out loud as he watched his God show His power. The demons looked afraid as the spirits couldn't escape their chosen jail. Next their two legs became one and thickened out into a trunk like shape. All three witches looked down at what once was their feet and legs. They soon realized what they were becoming and there was nothing they could do about it.

"Where is your master now?" Fr. Marc shouted at them. "See how he has abandoned you, he's nothing but empty promises."

They seemed to refuse to even look his way, much to his disappointment.

"My Lord, my God has heard my plea and come to save me and mankind from you and your evil."

They were either in a lot of pain and because of this, were ignoring him or they couldn't hear him at all. Fr. Marc looked behind him and saw Leo, Matthew and Noah head towards him, where he lay. It was still pouring down, from the heavens, with rain. The smell in the air was a magical one - it smelt of roses. Fr. Marc recognised this familiar smell, as he had encountered it many times before. This is the renowned smell which always happens after a successful exorcism. The boys' fathers were behind them, calling the villagers back to see the show (it's not every day you see witches turned into trees).

By now, as Fr. Marc turned back to observe the witches, he could see that their chests - up to their necks, had bulked out into the main part of the tree. Their arms then split and split again, over and over and turned into the several branches of the tree. Even their finger's divided up numerous times into the tree's twig ends. With only their heads left, the tree twisted a sinister way that made it hideously ugly and evil looking. At last glance, Fr. Marc caught sight of the most evil demon witch, Dragoona.

He saw with his own eyes, the fear inside hers. Her eyes were shaped like an angry dragon and he would remember that image of her forever. Her eyes had gone completely black and soulless, full of hate and revenge. This told him his God had worked quickly enough, but that the demons hadn't left her or the others and were still very much inside all of their bodies. The demons were cursed too, to be trees for however long God wished, along with the witches they had corrupted. They all watched as the trees grew into sinister shapes and so, finally, consuming all of what once were the witches.

All of a sudden it stopped raining; for some reason this made Fr. Marc sad. He couldn't explain why at the time and for some bizarre reason he had an urge to dig - dig down, deep into the mud the rain had created and hide himself away. He was so tired and planned to sleep for a week before he made his journey back home to Rome. He had an awful lot of explaining to do to the Pope.

He would help get his friend restored as head of the church. He called out to Leo, who was the nearest to him, and was suddenly shocked at how tall he looked, "He's like a giant now!" Leo didn't hear him at first and then Fr.

Marc heard them shouting. All three of the boys were calling out his name. There was panic in their voices as he watched them search everywhere for him. He called out again, louder, and then for the first time saw his hands. Only they were no longer human hands but the small digits or webs of a newt!

It suddenly dawned on poor Fr. Marc that he had been turned into a lizard. His worst nightmare had come true - the witch Dragoona had placed a curse on him just before the end. Oh dear God! What was he to do? He remembered then, all the thoughts, that only a few moments ago had been running wildly around in his head. How he had begged for time (a thousand years to be precise); that he wished he could rest and he even remembered thinking about trees and then wondered what spell she was concocting towards him. He even had thoughts that she could be trying to turn him into a lizard. He remembered all his panicking thoughts and now it all seemed to have come true. That's how he knew the curse would last for a thousand years. This he knew in his heart.

Many thoughts were racing through Fr. Marc's head as he was nearly stood on by Leo;

swiftly he moved, just in time, from being crushed into the mud.

"Hey watch where you're treading young man, you could have killed me!"

"Fr Marc is that you? Where are you?"

"Look down!"

Leo looked down towards the ground and where the voice was coming from. He then spotted a little newt on a muddy patch of grass. He knew, before he saw the newt move its mouth to speak, that it was Fr. Marc. The newt had the same piercing blue eyes as Fr. Marc, but still he rubbed his eyes in disbelief.

"Don't look so surprised young Leo, we were dealing with wicked old witches after all. They have clearly cursed me. I should thank myself lucky, as it could have been so much worse, don't you think? I could have been turned into a toad!"

Leo didn't know how to reply to this, but chose instead to sit down beside Fr. Marc and call his cousins over to see for themselves.

"FOUND HIM!"

"Where is he then?" Asked Noah.

"Here!"

Both Noah and Matthew look down into Leo's hand and see that their cousin is holding a little newt. Their minds ponder on what this means.

"Yes it's true, your cousin here has found me and I am now a delightful little lizard, thanks to those tree-witches over there and their curse."

Both Matthew and Noah followed the same action as Leo by rubbing their eyes. They had just seen the newt's mouth move and heard it speak. This was all a bit much to take in. So both lads joined their cousin and sat down. After some time they all carried him back to the village in triumph and wonder.

All the villagers came out to see him, as the three boys explained to their fathers and mothers what had happened to poor Fr. Marc. The people pledged a promise to him that they would always protect him and help him find a cure, no matter how long it took.

Fr Marc unofficially became the village mascot and priest. They all welcomed him into their fold. It was all agreed that he be kept a secret for his own protection, as they all knew now at first-hand how dangerous and powerful witches are and there could be hundreds more like them out there. That night the village celebrated overcoming the demon witches and Fr. Marc was their honoured guest. Leo, Matthew and Noah were hailed as heroes by everyone.

Fr. Marc and the three boys ventured back the next day into the woods, to the witches cabin, in search of a cure for the curse. Even in the daytime the cabin was scary and creepy and all of them were on edge. They all knew that it was highly likely for there to be many more witches out there, after Fr. Marc explained to them that the witches were part of a coven that they started. Many other women like them had joined up to practice witchcraft, so they always needed to be on guard. For all they knew, they could be close by and may intend on visiting the witches who once stayed here, not knowing what had become of them.

The cabin still smelled as foul as it did before. They came across so many children's clothes and tiny shoes. They found lots of different chains and traps - they soon discovered a trap door on the floor of the cabin. Together they lifted it up to find a staircase. It was very dark down there and so they lit a torch. Leo lead the way with Fr. Marc riding in his chest pocket. This hiding place was full of human bones and, lined up all along the far wall, were rows upon rows of cages full of dead and half dead animals. There were wolves, foxes, snakes and rats. Most were dead but a few of the wolves and snakes were alive. Fr. Marc explained to the boys that the witches would have used their blood and bodies in rituals and sacrifices. They decided to let them free, they were all too weak to attack them it was just too cruel to leave them to die there.

In the witches kitchen they found many oils and ointments, some potions and their big daunting spell book. There was also some books about vampires and werewolves that looked very interesting. The boys thought to themselves that most fairy tales must have always had some truth to them.

They didn't find anything in the spell book about cures. Fr. Marc accepted that it was a long shot. Just before they left the cabin and headed back home to their village, Matthew found another book. A strange creepy looking book with teeth attached to it and real hair. They all gathered around Matthew as he opened it up and read out loud the first page.

"This here book of origin and dreams belongs to the witch Dragoona, whoever shall read of it, whose eyes are not of her own, shall be ever cursed into the depths of hell itself."

Matthew reacted to this by dropping the book shut on the floor, as if the book itself were hot to touch.

"We need to burn this book, I could feel the evil in it."

"Listen young men, do not be afraid of a book, that is all it is. It is simply a book of her story, like a diary of her life - years and events. It's very common for them to do this and write some threat inside the first page to put off anyone whose eyes shouldn't see it."

"But Fr. Marcimus it could be true, look what she did to you. I, for one, don't want to know what's in there and I am never gonna hold that book again. That book is pure evil."

"Okay, let's take it back to the village and I alone will read it, learn all I can about her and then one of you will help bury it where no-one on earth will ever find it. My solid oath to you I swear."

So they all agreed. Once they got back to the village they heard news that came from all over the land and sea. The news was that many different women, some poor, some rich, some old, some young, were turning into trees, just like the witches did.

One tale was that it even happened in the streets of London. Another was about a woman in Egypt, holding a little boy's hand and taking him down to the river Nile to wash him, who just suddenly turned into a tree. As all the villagers gathered around to listen to the news, more men were arriving back to the village with more tales of women changing into trees. One woman was even on a boat sailing for Norway, she had three little boys with her, when everyone on board saw her transform into a living tree. They had to push her overboard into the water or they would have sunk.

Fr. Marc explained to everyone that this must be the other members of the witches coven. He made them see that they were all part of the same group of witches practicing witchcraft. Because of that, they had sealed their own fate with God. Now, along with the three Tree-Witches, they knew, they too were cursed to be Tree-Witches. Who knows how many there will be in the end. He suddenly thanked the Lord that they had found the book belonging to Dragoona back at the cabin. This meant, with any luck, he could work out just how many women were part of their coven. He knew it was a larger group of women than normal, because of their desire to take over and attain power.

Chapter 10
The Truth's Out!

11th of July 2014
Dear Journal,

Well! The cat is well and truly out of the bag now as Kristian, my best friend, has discovered the truth. Well, he's not stupid and he suspected something was very weird with me for a while now. He knows about Fr. Marc and I knew I couldn't keep it a secret forever.

He just happened to pop over the other day, it was to ask me to explain some homework to him that we got from our horrible math teacher Mrs Allen. Kristian is very good at maths and knows that I always struggle a bit. He decided to come over and pretend he didn't understand any of it, but really it was to offer to help me. I didn't hear him come in as my brother David met him out on the doorstep, on his way to the shops.

David let him in and told him I was in the den, and to head on in and find me. Oh, find me he did - talking to my pet newt. What a shock for poor Kristian when he heard Fr Marc talking back to me. He just stood there, he told me after. He was dumbfounded and listened to our conversation for a few minutes until he came to his senses and thought he had better let me know he was standing right there. To say we were shocked, me and Fr. Marc, would be true. We were also in such a good mood the pair of us because we were talking about a bird that nearly flew away with Fr. Marc earlier that day, while I was at school. He was telling me the whole story and we were both laughing as he said he punched the bird hard on the beak and it flew away without it's dinner. When we finally realised that Kristian was standing there, we couldn't help but burst into laughter again due to the look on Kristian's face.

He was clearly in shock and I sat him down on the most comfy chair in our 'seen better days' play den. Once I got him all cosy and settled, I explained that I had wanted to tell him for months. It wasn't my secret to share I explained - I hoped he could understand that. He managed a nod in my direction but never took his eyes off Fr. Marc, bless him.

Over the next few hours Fr Marc had explained nearly everything to him as he had done to me. I watched as Kristian, over those few hours, sat so still and listened. Then during the last hour he began to relax and asked Fr. Marc many questions - by the end he was over the shock. He was so very glad to be part of it all. He looked across at me at the end of it all and kindly said this to me.

"Your nana was some woman to keep this all to herself, it must have been so hard for her keeping this from you and David."

"My nana was the coolest of customers but the main thing for her, was the loyalty she showed towards Fr. Marc."

"Your nana understood, Kirah" said Fr. Marc, "I hope you both do too. If anyone discovers me I will be put into some god awful tank and experimented on for the rest of my life. They might even put me on show and get me to entertain people to make a fortune for themselves. I could never do that, I would rather die. Do you both understand this is all real, what I am sharing with you both. Most people don't believe in a God or a devil any more. So why would they care if we told them all about the Tree-Witches they would only dismiss you both for being mad and accuse you of teaching me to say these things."

Kirah replied "But come on, all the knowledge that you have from the past, that we couldn't possibly know. For heaven's sake, that would have to convince them we are telling the truth. How can we keep this a secret when we need people to prepare and fight, if those Tree-Witches do come back to life."

"Now listen to me Kristian, my friend, if I believed that any good would come from it and that we would all band together as good souls should, I would have revealed myself a long time ago. I didn't for a good reason, there are always going to be souls that will panic and those who will sell you out to the highest bidder. I know this because I have lived through it before. I know how some people will react to me. Some will declare that I'm an evil creature and should be destroyed."

Both me and Kristian gasp.

"You have to look at the bigger picture. If those Tree-Witches come back and wreak revenge then you can guarantee that most will panic and run. Some will even blame me and seek to hand me over to the Tree-Witches, in the hope the whole bad nightmare will go away and that they will be left alone. I know people, I have lived watching people for over a thousand years, dear boy. I am one of you and I know the fear that lies inside us. It doesn't always bring out the best in us. It usually, I hate to say it, brings out the worse in us and that's what the devil wants."

So both me and Kristian made a pledge to Fr. Marc, that we would keep it just amongst us for now and maybe later tell David and Claire and maybe our other friends (like Kristian's cousin Jack and the sister's across the road from me, Grace and Isabelle). For now it was between us three. I loved finally being able to share this secret with Kristian. I couldn't help thinking that maybe we would become really close and, just maybe, we would share our first kiss.

I know I'm too young to be thinking about boy's like that, but I can't help it, he's so sweet and kind to me. Kristian has always been the kind of friend who listens and takes in everything I am saying. He has never made fun of me in a cruel way, which boys sometimes do. If anyone dared, I know he would get into a fight over me. When I think like this I tell myself, I should forget about maybe becoming his girlfriend, because I would never want to lose him as a friend. He's just too special to me.

Chapter 11
Dragoona's Book!

14th of July,
Dear Journal,

We have found out so much stuff, that at times we wouldn't believe our own ears if it wasn't for the fact that I now have a talking newt - telling me things that make the hair stand up on the back of my neck. I don't know if I would have ever believed any of it. Kristian feels the same way. It's all so real now.

Learning about past history this way is mind boggling. To know that I descend from men who actually fought witches gives me an insight as to what we may face. I am starting to really wake up to the idea that we may have to fight them in the very near future.

One night, while my brother took Claire out to dinner, for the first time in weeks me and Fr. Marc, along with Kristian, went through my nana's hidden chest. He allowed me to look at some of the old books collected over the years. Suddenly, I just knew, the book - it was as if I could feel it throbbing and it was as though it was calling to me - the very same book which once belonged to Dragoona the Tree-Witch.

Fr. Marc told me that he had dug the book back up after Leo and Noah and Matthew had died. He knew that he would need it and the knowledge that was inside it. I could read it but only in his company, never alone, and that I should wear my rosary beads around my neck for protection. He gave Kristian my nana's spare ones to wear as well. He wouldn't go into detail but explained it was a dangerously evil book and it could, he believed, well, be cursed. He didn't want anything that may be was inside the book to affect me and my moral judgement. All he would say was that over his life time, some of my past ancestors were manipulated by the book and the words they read. They were the ones who had a weak faith and were not truly good souls.

It was not that they were seeking out the dark side or leaned more towards being bad. It was just a case of them being more easily corrupted and lead astray, than others would be. Fr. Marc said that we must never forget there is an ongoing war for our souls. We will, at times, be tempted by evil. The devil is always going to be there trying to weaken us and help us fail and ultimately make us lose our faith. That is what is all comes down to at the end of the day.

I hold the book and feel a little afraid of it. I wear my rosary beads which makes me feel safe. Half of me doesn't want to read the damned book. The other half of me is intrigued and dying to find out what's written in there. The way I look at is, I must know and learn all there is about the enemy that I will be facing, which isn't very far away now. I look across at Kristian and I can sense he feels the same way.

We found out yesterday, from Fr. Marc, the actual date and time the curse happened a thousand years ago. He said he would never forget it. It was on 14th of February (St. valentine's day!). The time was just after dawn, about 6 o'clock in the morning. He said one of the reasons he didn't forget that vital piece of information was because of the Pope. As you know, they had become good friends and he was worried for him as he had to flee Rome.

He later found out, many weeks after the curse on the witches and himself, some news from Rome. With great joy, his village had received word that the king of Germany, Henry

II, had in fact restored Pope Benedict VIII In Rome as their Pope and Head of the church. He had been supporting his friend and in return Pope Benedict VIII, to show his thanks, crowned him, Henry II - Holy Roman Emperor. He found out it had happened on the same day - 14th Feb. 1014. So he was never likely to forget. This was clearly another battle won against evil forces.

I thought about this and it scared me silly because that meant, we only had, about six months to prepare for this upcoming battle with the Tree-Witches (as they were known to me now). I welcomed Fr. Marc to stay with us, as myself and Kristian slowly opened up the book of the Tree-Witch Dragoona to read, I took a deep breath and suddenly felt the throbbing power the book possessed. This frightened me more than anything - I could feel all the hairs over my entire body stand to attention.

This truly was a book cursed with evil. I could feel some kind of force trying to read my thoughts and bend them. I was prepared for this, I simply whispered a small prayer to God to keep me safe and determinedly carried on reading. I felt Kristian reach out for my other hand. He held my hand so gently but firmly. This was going to be a small battle of minds. Mine and

Kristian's sane minds, against the evil twisted mind of hers - Dragoona.

I closed the book sharply and stared at it for a few minutes. How do you describe to someone just how hideously ugly this book is? Not only by the way it felt to hold in my hand, but also to look at. What on earth was it made from? Was that blood I could smell and were they real teeth I could see on the cover? In my nervous excitement I had failed to really take in the aura of the book. But on the edges of my mind I could feel a very strange sensation of pulling and pushing. Was it possible for this book to corrupt both mine and Kristian's minds? I was so very frightened and freaked out, but this had to be done. There was just no other way of understanding what we were up against, unless we read this damned book of hers together.

Fr. Marc explained that she had written everything down, about her past life and her new life, of how she had become a witch, and why. How she had met her sisters in witchcraft. Why and how they had become witches - all of it! What an exciting read this is going to be - fascinating but scary, this is her tale and the tale of her so called sisters, Serpentina and Hogonna..........................

Read my next journal if you want to find more.

End of book one.

Special thanks go to all my family and friends in life and on Facebook! Thank you all for supporting me and cheering me on. I will never forget all your support and kind words. Two special thanks' go out to my dear friend Beth and her lovely mum Jan for proof reading my book, I'd be lost without you.
Thank you Jules for being the perfect best friend and making sure that I keep my feet firmly on the ground, whilst my head is in the clouds!
I could not have done it without you.
XXXXXXXXXXXXXXXXXXXXXX

Printed in Great Britain
by Amazon.co.uk, Ltd.,
Marston Gate.